THIS WALKER BOOK BELONGS TO:

_____

_____

_____

for Sebastian with all my love

'de te fabula narratur'

First published 1992 by Walker Books Ltd
87 Vauxhall Walk, London SE11 5HJ

This edition published 2004

2 4 6 8 10 9 7 5 3

The right of Debi Gliori to be identified as author/illustrator
of this work has been asserted by her in accordance
with the Copyright, Designs and Patents Act 1988

This book has been typeset in Garamond

Printed in China

British Library Cataloguing in Publication Data:
a catalogue record for this book is available
from the British Library

ISBN 1-84428-784-X

www.walkerbooks.co.uk

When I'm Big

Debi Gliori

WALKER BOOKS
AND SUBSIDIARIES
LONDON • BOSTON • SYDNEY • AUCKLAND

When I'm big, I'm going to stay up as late as I like and make myself marshmallows on toast instead of going to bed.

When I'm big, I'm going swimming with the whales in the deep blue sea instead of puddling about in the bath.

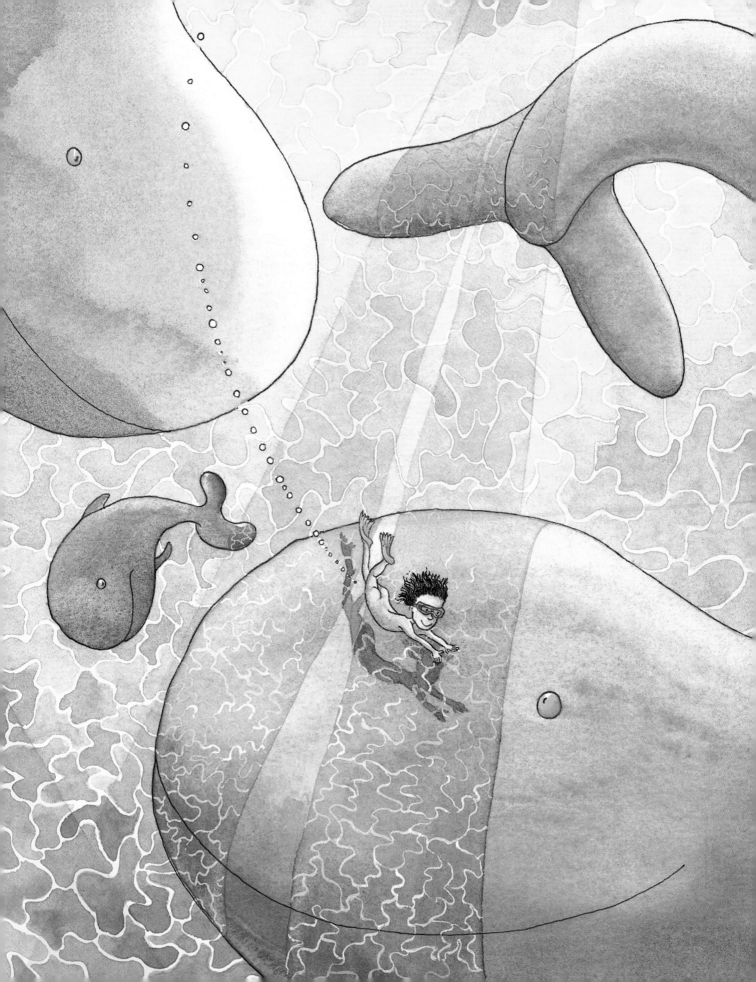

When I'm big, I'm going to wear a bird-suit and gumboots all day long instead of a jumper and dungarees.

When I'm big,
I'm going to
have a huge
back garden
with sand
mountains that
touch the sky
and a lake in
the middle
instead of a
sandpit and a
paddling pool.

When I'm big, I'm going to drive the trolley round the shops with Dad in it instead of the other way round.

When I'm big,
I'm going to
grow triffids and
Venus fly-traps
and man-eating
orchids instead of
mustard and cress.

When I'm big I'm going to ride a proper bike instead of a tricycle.

When I'm big,
I'm going to have
twelve lions, two
tigers, a bunch of
grizzly bears and
a shark instead of
a dog, a cat and
a goldfish.

When I'm big,
I'm going to put
Mum and Dad
to bed and read
them a story and
turn out the light
and go downstairs
on my own.

I can squeeze
into the safest
place in the world.